Favorite Fairy Tales

TOLD IN RUSSIA

Favorite Fairy Tales

TOLD IN RUSSIA

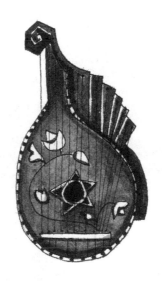

Retold from Russian Storytellers

by Virginia Haviland

Illustrated by Kim Howard

A Beech Tree Paperback Book *New York*

First Beech Tree Edition, 1995, published by arrangement with Little, Brown and Co.
Printed in the United States of America

10 9 8 7 6 5 4 3 2 1

These stories have been adapted from the following sources:

"To Your Good Health," from the *Crimson Fairy Book* by Andrew Lang (New York, Longmans, Green and Company, Inc., 1903).

"Vasilisa the Beautiful," from a literal translation, by Harry Andrews, of the Russian of Alexei Afanasèv (Moscow, Government Publishing House, 1957 [original compilation 1855]).

"Snegourka, the Snow Maiden," from *Folk-Lore and Legends, Russian and Polish*, edited by "C.S.P." (London, Gibbings, 1890; Philadelphia, J.B. Lippincott Company, 1891).

"The Straw Ox," from *Cossack Fairy Tales and Folk Tales*, selected, edited, and translated from the Ruthenian, by R. Nisbet Bain (London, Lawrence and Bullen, 1894).

"The Flying Ship," from *Russian Fairy Tales*, selected and translated from *The Skazki of Polevoi*, by R. Nisbet Bain (London, Lawrence and Bullen, 1892).

Library of Congress Cataloging-in-Publication Data

Haviland, Virginia, 1911-1988
  Favorite fairy tales told in Russia / retold from Russian storytellers by Virginia Haviland ; illustrated by Kim Howard.
    p. cm.
  Originally published: 1st ed. Boston : Little, Brown, 1961.
  Contents: To your good health — Vasilisa the Beautiful — Snegourka, the Snow Maiden — The straw ox — The flying ship
  ISBN 0-688-12603-0 (paper)
  1. Fairy tales — Russia. [1. Fairy tales. 2. Folklore — Russia.]
I. Howard, Kim, ill. II. Title. III. Title: Told in Russia.
PZ8.H295Favr 1995
[398.2'094701]—dc20   94–21521
                        CIP
                        AC

Minor editorial and style changes have been made in the stories for these new editions.

Contents

Favorite Fairy Tales

TOLD IN RUSSIA

To Your Good Health

To Your Good Health

L ONG, LONG AGO there lived a Tsar who was such a mighty ruler that whenever he sneezed he expected everyone in his kingdom to say "To your good health!" Everyone said it, except a shepherd with bright blue eyes. He would not say it.

The Tsar heard of this and was very angry. He sent for the shepherd to come before him.

13

The shepherd came at once. He stood before the throne, where the Tsar sat looking very grand and powerful. But grand and powerful as the Tsar might be, the shepherd was not one bit afraid of him.

"Say at once, 'To my good health!'" cried the Tsar.

"To my good health!" replied the shepherd.

"To *mine*—to *mine*, you rascal!" stormed the Tsar.

"To mine, to mine, Your Majesty," was the answer.

"But to *mine*—to my *own*," roared the Tsar and beat on his breast in a rage.

"Well, yes; to mine, of course, to my own," cried the shepherd and gently tapped his breast.

The Tsar was beside himself with fury. He could not think what to do.

The Lord Chamberlain whispered to the shepherd, "Say at once—say this very moment: 'To your health, Your Majesty.' If you don't say it, you will lose your life."

"No, I won't say it till I get your daughter, the Tsarevna, for my wife," said the shepherd.

The Tsarevna was sitting on a little throne beside the Tsar. She looked as lovely as a little golden dove. When she heard what the shepherd said, she could not help laughing. This young shepherd pleased her very much. Indeed, he pleased her better than any Tsar's son she had yet seen.

But the Tsar was not as pleasant as his daughter. He gave orders to throw the shepherd into the white bear's pit. So guards led him away and thrust him into the pit with the white bear—a bear who had eaten nothing for two days and was very hungry.

The door of the pit was hardly closed before the bear rushed at the shepherd. But when it saw the shepherd's eyes it shrank away into a corner and gazed at him from there. It did not dare to touch him. Instead it sucked its own paws from sheer hunger.

The shepherd knew that if he took his eyes off the beast he would be killed. To keep himself awake while he held the bear with his eyes, he made up songs and sang them.

Thus the night went by.

Next morning the Lord Chamberlain came, expecting to see the shepherd's bones. He was amazed to find him alive and well!

He led him back to the Tsar, who fell into a furious temper and said, "Well, you have learned what it is to be very near death. Now will you say, 'To my good health'?"

But the shepherd answered, "I am not afraid of ten deaths. I will only say it if I may have the Tsarevna for my wife."

"Then go to your death," cried the Tsar. He ordered him to be thrown into a den with wild boars.

The wild boars had not been fed for a week. When the shepherd was thrust into their den, they rushed at him to tear him to pieces. But the shepherd took a little flute from his sleeve and began to play a merry tune. At first the wild boars shrank away. Then they got up on their hind legs and danced gaily.

They looked so funny that the shepherd would have given anything to be able to laugh. But he dared not stop playing. He knew well enough that the moment he stopped, the boars would fall upon him and tear him to pieces. His eyes were of no use to him here, for he could not have stared ten wild boars in the face all at the same time. So he kept on playing. The wild boars danced slowly until he began to play faster. Then they could hardly twist and turn quickly enough. Faster and faster he played until the boars fell over each other in a heap, breathless and worn out.

At last the shepherd dared to laugh. He laughed long and loud. When the Lord Chamberlain came early in the morning, expecting to find only his bones, tears of laughter were still running down his cheeks.

★ ★ ★

As soon as the Tsar was dressed, the shepherd was again brought before him. The Tsar was more angry than ever to think the wild boars had not torn the shepherd to bits.

He said to him, "Well, you have learned how it feels to be near ten deaths. Now say, 'To my good health'!"

The shepherd simply replied, "I do not fear a hundred deaths. I will say it only if I may have the Tsarevna for my wife."

"Then go to a hundred deaths!" roared the Tsar, and he ordered the shepherd to be thrown down the deep Well of Knives.

The guards dragged him away to a dark dungeon. In the middle of it was a deep well with long, sharp knife blades sticking out all around it. At the bottom of the well was a little light to show when anyone thrown in had fallen to the bottom.

When they came to the dungeon, the shepherd begged the guards to leave him alone a little while so that he might look down into the well. Perhaps he might, after all, make up his mind to say "To your good health!" to the Tsar.

So the guards left him alone. The shepherd stuck up his long stick near the well. He hung his cloak around it and put his hat on the top. He also hung his knapsack inside the cloak so that it might seem to have a body within it. When all this was done, he called out to the guards. He said that he had considered the matter but, after all, he could not say what the Tsar wished.

The guards came in. But the shepherd had hidden in a dark corner. They threw the hat and cloak, knapsack and stick, all down the well together. They looked to see that the light went out at the bottom, and they left. They each thought this really was the end of the shepherd. But he was laughing to himself all the time.

★ ★ ★

Quite early next morning, in came the Lord Chamberlain, carrying a lamp. He nearly fell over backward with surprise when he saw the shepherd alive and well.

When the Lord Chamberlain brought the shepherd to the throne, the Tsar's fury was greater than ever. He cried out, "Well, now that you have been near a hundred deaths, will you say, 'To your good health'?"

But the shepherd only gave the same answer. "I won't say it until the Tsarevna is my wife."

"Perhaps after all you may do it for less," said the Tsar. He saw that there was no chance of doing away with the shepherd, so he ordered his coachman to drive himself and the shepherd to the silver wood.

When they reached it, the Tsar said: "Do you see this wood? Well, if you will say 'To your good health,' I will give it to you."

The shepherd became hot and cold by turns, but he persisted: "I will not say it until the Tsarevna is my wife."

The Tsar was much vexed. He drove farther on until they came to a splendid castle, all of gold, and then he said:

"Do you see this golden castle? Well, I will give you that too, both the silver wood and the golden castle, if only you will say that one thing to me, 'To your good health.'"

The shepherd gazed and wondered. He was quite dazzled, but he only said, "No, I will not

say it until I have the Tsarevna for my wife."

The Tsar was overwhelmed with feeling. He gave orders to drive on to the diamond pond. There he tried once more.

"Do you see this diamond pond? I will give you that too, the silver wood and the golden castle and the diamond pond. You shall have them all—all—if you will but say 'To your good health'!"

The shepherd had to shut his eyes tight not to be dazzled by the brilliant pond. But still he said, "No, no; I will not say it until I have the Tsarevna for my wife."

The Tsar saw, then, that all his efforts were useless. He might as well give in. So he said, "Well, well, it's all the same to me. I will give you my daughter. But, then, you really and truly must say to me, 'To your good health'!"

"Of course I'll say it. Why should I not say it? It stands to reason that I shall say it then."

At this the Tsar was more delighted than anyone could have believed. He made it known all through the country that there was to be great rejoicing. The Tsarevna was going to be married.

And everyone did rejoice that the Tsarevna, who had refused so many royal suitors, had fallen in love with the blue-eyed shepherd.

There was such a wedding as had never been seen before. Everyone ate and drank and danced. Even the sick feasted, and all newborn children were given presents.

The greatest merrymaking was in the Tsar's palace. There the best bands played and the best food was cooked. A crowd of people sat down to feast, and all was fun and merrymaking.

According to custom, a great roasted boar's head was carried in and placed before the Tsar. The savory smell of the meat was so strong that the Tsar began to sneeze with all his might.

"To your very good health!" cried the shepherd before anyone else. And the Tsar was so delighted that he did not regret having given him his daughter.

In time, when the old Tsar died, the shepherd succeeded him. He made a very good ruler and never expected his people to wish him well against their will. All the same, everyone did wish him well, for they all loved him.

Vasilisa the Beautiful

Vasilisa the Beautiful

O NCE UPON A TIME a merchant and his wife had an only daughter. She was so lovely to look at that she was called Vasilisa the Beautiful.

When Vasilisa was eight years old her mother called her to her bedside one day.

"I am dying, Vasilisa, my dear. I leave you my blessing and this little doll. Listen now and remember what I say. You must keep this little doll with you always, and be sure you do not show it to any other person. If any trouble comes your way, you must feed this doll and ask its advice, and it will tell you what to do."

After his wife died, the merchant grieved and was lonely, but a time came when he thought of marrying again. At length he decided on a widow, no longer young, who had two daughters a little older than Vasilisa. He thought the widow would make a good mother for his Vasilisa—but he was wrong.

Because Vasilisa was the most beautiful girl in the village, the stepmother and the sisters were jealous. They ordered her to do all the hardest work, hoping she would become tired and sickly and would be burned dark by the sun and the wind. Instead, Vasilisa became even more beautiful, while the stepmother and the sisters became thinner and uglier, just from ill temper.

Now, the good little doll was helping Vasilisa with her work. From her scanty food, she always saved the tastiest morsels for her doll. At night, when everyone clse had gone to bed, Vasilisa would go into her closet and lift the tiny doll out of her pocket.

"Here, my little dolly, eat and listen," she would say. Then she would describe how her evil stepmother and the sisters were treating her. "Tell me what I must do!" she would beg. The little doll comforted her with smiles and good advice. And every morning she did all of Vasilisa's tasks. While Vasilisa rested in the garden or picked flowers as the doll told her to do, all the flower beds were weeded, the cabbages were watered, the fire laid, and the water jugs filled. This way Vasilisa had a good and easy life.

As Vasilisa grew up, every young man in the village admired her and wanted her for his bride. No young man even looked at Vasilisa's stepsisters. This made the stepmother meaner than ever. She told every one of the suitors, "I

will not give the youngest in marriage before I give the elders."

The suitors would go away, while the stepmother showed her anger by beating poor Vasilisa.

One day the merchant went away on business, to be gone for a long time. The stepmother at once moved into a different house near a dense forest. She knew that in a clearing deep in the forest stood a small hut, and in that hut lived Baba Yaga. This Baba Yaga was a wicked witch. She ate people as if they were chickens.

As soon as the stepmother had settled into the new house, she began sending Vasilisa out into the forest. But Vasilisa never once became lost. Her little doll always showed her the way home and did not let her go near Baba Yaga's hut.

Autumn came and the days were shorter. In the evenings the stepmother gave out work to the three girls. One was to make lace, the second was to knit stockings, and Vasilisa was to spin. Each had a certain amount to do before going to bed. One night the stepmother put out all the lights except one candle where the girls were working. Then she went off to sleep.

The girls worked on. The candle began to sputter, and one of the sisters took up the snuffers as if to trim the wick. But, as her mother had ordered her to do, she put the candle out, instead.

"What shall we do now?" the sisters cried. "There is no fire to light the candle, and our tasks are not finished. We shall have to go and get a light from Baba Yaga."

The one who was making lace said, "I will not have to go, for I have enough light shining from my needles."

"And I shall not go," said the one who was knitting, "for I, too, have enough light from my needles."

"You will have to go to Baba Yaga for the fire," said they to Vasilisa, and they pushed her from the room.

Vasilisa stole into her closet. She gave food to her little doll and whispered, "Dolly, dear, eat this and listen! My stepsisters are sending me to Baba Yaga the witch. She will eat me up!"

The little doll ate, and her eyes shone like lighted candles. "Do not be afraid, Vasilisa the Beautiful. Go where they send you, but keep me with you and Baba Yaga can do you no harm."

Vasilisa hid the doll again in her pocket. She crossed herself and walked bravely into the thick dark forest.

All through the night she walked. Then suddenly a horse and rider, all in white, rode past her, and it became light. As she walked on, another horseman, all in red, rode past, and the sun rose.

All that day Vasilisa continued through the forest, and by evening she arrived at the clearing. There was Baba Yaga's strange little house, standing on hen's legs. Around it circled a fence made of human bones, and on top of the fence sat a row of skulls.

Suddenly another rider appeared, dressed all in black. He rode up to the door and disappeared, and it was night. But the darkness did not last, for the eyes in the skulls lit up like lamps, and the clearing became as bright as day. Vasilisa, seeing this, stood frozen with terror.

Now a terrible noise sounded in the forest, with trees shaking and dry leaves rustling. Out of the forest Baba Yaga came riding in a mortar, driving it with a pestle, and sweeping away her tracks with her broom. She stopped at the gates to sniff the air and to cry out, "I smell a Russian! Who is here?"

Vasilisa, trembling with fear, went over to Baba Yaga and bowed low. "My stepmother's daughters have sent me to ask you for fire."

"Good!" said Baba Yaga. "Work for me for a while and I will give you fire. If you don't work, I shall eat you up."

Baba Yaga entered her house, whistling, with Vasilisa following. Baba Yaga lay down on her couch and commanded, "Bring me whatever is in the oven. I want to eat."

Vasilisa, summoning her courage, lit a taper from one of the skulls and brought to Baba Yaga the food from the oven. It was enough for ten men. And from the cellar she brought drink. Baba Yaga ate and drank until only a small crust of bread and a tiny bit of meat was left for hungry Vasilisa.

Baba Yaga, ready for bed, said to Vasilisa, "Tomorrow, when I go out, you are to clear the yard, sweep the house, do the washing, and get my dinner. You must be sure that everything is done before I come home, or I shall eat you up."

As soon as she had commanded all this, Baba Yaga began to snore.

Vasilisa put the last crumbs of supper before her little doll and said, "Here, dolly, eat this and listen to my sorrow. Baba Yaga has given me hard tasks to do, and she threatens to eat me if I don't finish them before she comes home tomorrow. Help me, please!"

"Vasilisa, my beautiful, do not be afraid. Say your prayers and go to bed. The morning is wiser than the evening."

Very early the next day, Vasilisa arose. The lights in the skulls flickered out. The white rider passed, and it was dawn. Baba Yaga left the house and whistled. Her mortar and pestle and broom appeared at once.

The red horseman rode by, and the sun came out. Baba Yaga sat in her mortar and went off, driving it with the pestle while she swept away her tracks with the broom.

Vasilisa looked about Baba Yaga's house and wondered at her wealth. She stood still, not knowing what part of the work she should do first. But when she looked again, the work was already done.

"Oh, my good helper!" said Vasilisa. "You have saved me!"

As she climbed back into Vasilisa's pocket, the little doll said, "All you have to do now is to set out Baba Yaga's dinner."

Towards evening Vasilisa put everything on the table and waited for Baba Yaga. It began to grow dark. The black horseman rode by, and it became completely dark, except that the eyes in the skulls were now alight.

Suddenly Vasilisa heard the trees shake and the leaves rustle. Baba Yaga swept in and Vasilisa met her.

"Is everything done?" Baba Yaga demanded.

"Look for yourself, granny!" said Vasilisa.

Baba Yaga looked. She was vexed that she could find no fault. "All right, Vasilisa."

Baba Yaga ate her supper and prepared to go to sleep. But first she commanded, "Tomorrow you must do everything as you did today." Then Baba Yaga turned to the wall and began to snore.

Vasilisa fed her little doll and the doll told her, as it had the day before, "Pray to God, and go to sleep. The morning is wiser than the evening. Everything shall be done, Vasilisa the Beautiful."

In the morning Baba Yaga whistled again, and her mortar and pestle and broom appeared at once. The red horseman rode by, and the sun rose in the sky. Baba Yaga climbed into the mortar and was off, sweeping away her traces as before.

The little doll performed all the tasks again, while Vasilisa wondered at the magic. That evening Baba Yaga began to eat her great supper, while Vasilisa sat silently.

"Why do you not speak to me? Why do you sit there as if you were dumb?"

"I do not dare to say anything, but if you will permit it I should like to ask something."

"Ask, if you will, but know that not every question leads to something good. If you know much, you are soon old."

"I should like to ask you about what I saw as I came here. First I was overtaken by a rider in white on a white horse. Who was he?"

"He is my bright day."

"Then there came a rider dressed in red on a red horse. Who was he?"

"He is my red sun."

"And who is the black rider who overtook me at your very door?"

"That is my dark night. All of these are my faithful servants."

Vasilisa was silent.

"Why don't you ask me more?" said Baba Yaga.

"That is enough for me. You said yourself, granny, that if you know much, you are soon old."

"It is good that you asked only about things you saw outside. I do not like stories carried out of my house. I eat those who are too curious."

Baba Yaga herself now asked, "How do you manage to finish all the work I give you?"

"I am helped by my mother's blessing!"

"Her *blessing*! Get out of here as fast as you can, blessed daughter! I want no one near me who is blessed!"

She pushed Vasilisa to the door. Then she took one of the skulls with the burning eyes, put it on a stick, and handed it to Vasilisa. "Take this fire. It is what your stepmother's daughters sent you for."

Vasilisa ran off by the light of the skull, and by evening of the next day she was out of the forest. Thinking they could not still be without fire, she was about to throw the skull away when a deep voice said, "Don't throw me away. Take me to your stepmother."

Vasilisa saw no light in her stepmother's house. She decided to take the skull inside. The sisters met her and seemed friendly. They told her that from the day Vasilisa had gone, they had had no fire. Any that they borrowed from their neighbors went out as soon as they brought it into the house.

"But perhaps your fire may last!" said the stepmother.

They carried the skull inside. Its eyes stared and stared at the stepmother and her daughters, and they could not hide from them. By morning Vasilisa was alone in the house. The others had burned to cinders.

Vasilisa quickly buried the skull and locked the house. She went into the town and asked a poor old woman who lived alone to give her a home until her father should come back.

All went well now, except that Vasilisa did not have enough to do. One day she asked the old woman, "Please buy me some of the very best flax. I should like to do some spinning."

The old woman brought home some very good flax, and Vasilisa set to work. She worked so well that her thread came as fine as hair. It piled up until Vasilisa knew she must start weaving. But no loom was good enough for such fine thread.

Vasilisa thought again of her doll. The little doll was ready, and said, "I will take care of everything. Please bring me a comb, a spindle, a shuttle, and some horsehair." And sure enough, during the night, while Vasilisa slept, the little · doll made a splendid loom for weaving.

By the end of the winter all of the thread was woven into linen. It was so fine that it could be pulled through the eye of a needle, like thread itself. Vasilisa handed this beautiful linen to the old woman. "Sell this cloth, granny, and keep for yourself whatever money it brings."

The old woman looked at the cloth and was amazed.

"No, my child! This I shall not sell. Such linen as this should be worn only by the Tsar. I will take it to the palace."

Off she went, and soon the Tsar saw her walking up and down past his windows.

"What do you want, old woman?" he asked.

"Your Almighty Highness, I have something wonderful which I wish to show only to you."

The Tsar gave orders for the old woman to be

admitted. When he saw the linen, he, also, was astounded.

"What do you want for it?" he asked.

"There is no price, Your Majesty. I have brought it as a gift."

The Tsar decided to have shirts made out of the linen, but no seamstress could be found who was skillful enough to handle such cloth as this.

Finally the Tsar asked the old woman to come back to the palace. He said to her, "If you were able to weave such linen as this, you should also be able to make it into shirts."

"It wasn't I who wove this linen, Your Majesty. It was my foster child who spun and wove it."

"Well, then, let her sew the shirts!"

All of this the old woman carried home and repeated to Vasilisa.

"I knew this would happen," said Vasilisa. And

she locked herself in her little room and began
to sew. She sewed on and on without stopping
until she had a dozen shirts finished.

The woman carried the shirts to the Tsar.
Vasilisa stayed at home and washed and combed
and dressed herself. Then she sat down at the
window to see what would happen next.

Soon a servant appeared and said, "His

Majesty the Tsar would see the clever seamstress who has made him such fine shirts. He
wishes to reward her with his own hands."

Vasilisa the Beautiful went before the Tsar.
And as soon as he saw her, he fell head over
heels in love with her. He took Vasilisa by the
hand, sat her near him, and ordered bells to be
rung for their wedding.

Soon now Vasilisa's father returned, and discovered the good fortune that had at last come to his daughter. Vasilisa took him, and the old woman also, to live in the palace. And the little doll she carried ever after in her pocket.

Snegourka,
the Snow Maiden

Snegourka,
the Snow Maiden

ONCE UPON A TIME a peasant named Ivan had a wife called Marousha. They had been married many years, but they had no children. This was a great sorrow to them. In fact, their only pleasure was watching the children of their neighbors.

One winter day, when fresh white snow lay deep everywhere, Ivan and Marousha watched the children playing in it, laughing loudly as they played. The children began to make a beautiful snow man, and Ivan and Marousha enjoyed seeing it grow.

All of a sudden Ivan said, "Wife, let us go out and make a snow man, too!"

Marousha was ready. "Why not?" she said. "We may as well amuse ourselves a little. But why should we make a big snow man? Let us make a snow child, since God has not given us a living one."

"You are right," said Ivan. He led his wife outdoors.

There in the garden by their house they set to work to make a child of snow. They made a little body, and little hands, and little feet. When all that was done, they rolled a snowball and shaped it into a head.

"Heaven bless you!" cried a passer-by.

"Thanks," replied Ivan.

"The help of Heaven is always good," said Marousha.

"What are you doing?" asked the passer-by.

"Look," said Ivan.

"We are making a snow girl," said Marousha.

On the ball of snow which stood for a head they put a nose and a chin, and they made two little holes for eyes.

Just as they finished their work—oh, wonderful!—the little snow maiden moved! Ivan felt a warm breath come from her lips. He drew back, and looked. The snow maiden's sparkling eyes were blue. Her lips, rosy now, curved in a lovely smile.

"What is this?" cried Ivan, making the sign of the cross.

The snow maiden bent her head, and the snow fell from now golden hair, which curled about her soft round cheeks. She moved her little arms and legs in the snow as if she were a real child.

"Ivan! Ivan!" cried Marousha. "Heaven has heard our prayers." She threw herself on the child and covered her with kisses.

"Ah, Snegourka, my own dear snow maiden," she cried, and she carried her into the house.

Ivan had much to do to recover from his surprise. Marousha became foolish with joy.

Hour by hour Snegourka, the snow maiden, grew both in size and in beauty. Ivan and Marousha could not take their eyes away from her.

The little house, which had held such sadness, was now full of life and merriment. The neighboring children came to play with the little snow maiden. They chattered with her and sang songs to her, teaching her all they knew.

The snow maiden was very clever. She noticed everything, and learned quickly. When she spoke, her voice was so sweet that one could have gone on listening to it for ever. She was gentle, obedient, and loving. In turn, everyone loved her. She played in the snow with the others, and they saw how well her little hands could model things of snow and ice.

Marousha said, "See what joy Heaven has given us in our old age."

"Heaven be thanked," replied Ivan.

At last the winter came to an end, and the spring sun shone down and warmed the earth. The snow melted, green grass sprang up in the fields, and the lark sang high in the sky. The village girls went singing:

> *Sweet spring, how did you come to us?*
> *How did you come?*
> *Did you come on a plow, or on a harrow?*

Although the other children were gay with spring, and full of song and dance, the snow maiden sat by the window looking more and more sad.

"What is the matter with you, my dear child?" asked Marousha, drawing her close and caressing her. "Are you not well? You are not merry."

"It is nothing, Mother," answered the snow maiden. "I am quite well."

The last snow of the winter had now melted and disappeared. Flowers bloomed in every field and garden. In the forest, the nightingale poured out its song and all the world seemed glad, except the snow maiden, who became still sadder.

She would run away from her friends and hide from the sun in dark nooks, like a timid flower under the trees. She liked best to play by the water, under shady willow trees. She was happy at night and during a storm, even during a fierce hailstorm. When the sun broke forth again—when the hail melted—she began to weep.

Summer came, with ripening fields, and the Feast of Saint John was at hand. The snow maiden's friends begged her to go with them to the forest, to pick berries and flowers.

The snow maiden did not want to go, but her mother urged her, even though she, too, felt afraid.

"Go, my child, and play. And you, her friends, look well after her. You know how much I love her."

In the forest the children picked wild flowers and made themselves wreaths. It was warm, and they ran about singing, each wearing a crown of flowers.

"Look at us," they said to the snow maiden. "Look how we run! Follow us."

They went on, dancing and singing. Then all of a sudden they heard, behind them, a sigh. . . .

They looked. There was nothing to be seen. They looked again. The snow maiden was no longer among them.

They called out and shouted her name, but there was no answer.

"Where can she be? She must have gone home," they said.

Back they ran to the village, but no one there had seen her either.

During the next day and the day following, everyone searched. They went through the woods, and looked through every thicket, but no trace of the little snow maiden was to be found.

Ivan and Marousha felt their hearts were broken. For a long time Marousha would cry, "Snegourka, my sweet snow maiden, come to me!"

Sometimes Ivan and Marousha thought they could hear the voice of their child. Perhaps, when the snow returned, she would come back to them.

The Straw Ox

The Straw Ox

ONCE UPON A TIME there lived an old man and an old woman. The old man worked in the fields burning pitch pine to make tar, while the old woman sat at home and spun flax. They were so poor that all their earnings went for food, and nothing more.

At last the old woman had a good idea. "Look now, Husband," cried she. "Make me a straw ox, and smear it all over with tar."

"Why, you foolish woman!" said he. "What's the good of an ox of that sort?"

"Never mind," said she. "You just make it. I know what I am about."

What was the poor man to do? He set to work and made the ox of straw, then smeared it all over with tar.

The night passed away. At early dawn the old woman picked up her distaff for spinning and drove the straw ox out into the grassy steppe to graze. She sat herself down behind a hillock, began spinning her flax, and cried, "Graze away, little ox, while I spin my flax! Graze away, little ox, while I spin my flax!"

While she spun, her head drooped and she began to doze. And while she was dozing, from back of the huge pines a bear came rushing out upon the ox and said, "Who are you? Speak and tell me!"

And the ox answered, "A three-year-old heifer am I, made of straw and smeared with tar."

"Oh!" said the bear. "Stuffed with straw and trimmed with tar, are you? Give me some of your straw and tar, so that I may patch up my ragged fur again!"

"Take some," said the ox. So the bear fell upon the ox and began to tear at the tar. He tore and he tore, and he buried his teeth in the tar until he found he couldn't let go again. He tugged and he tugged, but it was no good. The ox slowly dragged him away.

The old woman awoke, and there was no ox to be seen.

"Alas, old fool that I am!" she cried. "But perhaps the ox has gone home."

She quickly caught up her distaff and hastened away. At home she saw that the ox had dragged the bear up to the fence.

"Husband, Husband!" she cried. "Look, look! The ox has brought us a bear! Come out and kill it!" The old man ran out. He tore the bear off the ox, tied him up, and threw him in the cellar.

★ ★ ★

Next morning, between dark and dawn, the old woman again took her distaff and drove the ox into the steppe to graze. She sat herself down by a mound, began spinning, and said, "Graze away, little ox, while I spin my flax! Graze away, little ox, while I spin my flax!"

While she spun, her head dropped and she dozed. And, lo! from back of the huge pines, a gray wolf came dashing out upon the ox and said, "Who are you? Come, tell me!"

"A three-year-old heifer am I, stuffed with straw and trimmed with tar," said the ox.

"Oh! Trimmed with tar, are you? Then give me some of your tar to tar my sides!"

"Take some," said the ox.

With that the wolf fell upon the ox and tried to tear away the tar. He tugged and tugged, and he tore with his teeth, but he could get none off. When he tried to let go, he couldn't. Tug and worry as he might, it was no good.

When the old woman awoke, there was no ox in sight. "But maybe my ox has gone home!" she cried. "I will go and see."

Again she was astonished. By the fence stood the ox, with the wolf still tugging at him. She called to her old man, who hurried to throw the wolf, also, into the cellar.

On the third day the old woman again drove her ox into the pasture to graze. She sat herself down by a mound and dozed off.

This time a fox came running up. "Who are you?" she asked the ox.

"I'm a three-year-old heifer, stuffed with straw and trimmed with tar."

"Give me some of your tar to smear my sides!"

"Take some," said the ox.

The fox thereupon fastened her teeth in him, but couldn't draw them out again.

The old man cast the fox into the cellar just as he had the bear and the wolf. And after that a hare was caught in the same way, and sent to join the other animals.

Now that he had all these animals safe in his cellar, the old man sat down on a bench and began sharpening a knife.

The bear called up to him, "Tell me, old man, why are you sharpening your knife?"

"To cut off your skin, so that I may make a leather jacket for myself and a cape for my wife."

"Oh! Don't skin me, old man! Let me go, and I promise I will bring you a hive of sweet honey."

"Honey? Very well, then, but be sure you bring it." And the old man unbound the bear and let him go.

Now the old man sat down on the bench again and began sharpening his knife.

This time the wolf asked, "Old man, why are you sharpening your knife?"

"To strip off your skin, so that I may make me a warm cap for the winter."

"Oh! Don't skin me, old man! I will bring you a whole flock of tender sheep."

"Well, see that you do it then." And the old man let the wolf go.

The old man sat down once more and began sharpening his knife.

This time the fox put out her little snout and asked him, "Be so kind, dear old man, as to tell me why you are sharpening your knife!"

"Little foxes," said the old man, "have fine skins that do nicely for collars and trimmings. I want to skin you!"

"Oh! Don't take my skin away, old man! I will bring you a feast of plump hens and geese."

"Very well, then. See that you do!" And he let the fox go.

The hare remained alone now, and the old man began sharpening his knife for him.

"Why do you do that?" asked the hare. The old man replied, "Little hares have nice soft skins, which will make me warm mittens for the winter."

"Oh! Don't skin me! I will bring you delicious kale and cauliflower, if only you will let me go!"

Well, the old man let the hare go also.

★ ★ ★

Very early the next morning, there came a buzzing noise at the doorway.

"Old man," cried the old woman, "there's someone scratching at our door. Go and see who it is!"

The old man went out. There he found the bear carrying a whole hive full of honey.

The old man took the honey from the bear.

And no sooner did he lie down again on his bed than he heard another noise.

The old man looked out and saw the wolf driving a flock of sheep into the yard. Close on his heels came the fox, driving before him geese and hens and other fowl. Last of all came the hare, bringing cauliflower and kale and other fresh vegetables.

Now the old man was happy, and the old woman was happy. The old man sold the sheep and the fowl for so much money that he needed nothing more. As for the straw ox, it stood in the sun until it fell to pieces.

The Flying Ship

The Flying Ship

ONCE UPON A TIME a man and his wife had three sons. Two sons were clever, but the third was a fool. The old woman loved the first two, and quite spoiled them, but she gave little of anything to the third.

One day a message came from the Tsar which said, "Whoever builds a ship that can fly, to him will I give my daughter, the Tsarevna, in marriage."

The elder brothers said at once that they must go and seek their fortunes, and they begged a blessing of their parents. Their mother got them ready for the journey, filling their packs with the best of food to eat on the way, and the best to drink, too.

The fool then began to beg to go, too. But his mother asked, "Where would *you* go, Fool? Why, the wolves would devour you!"

But the fool kept insisting, "I will go, I will go!" Finally his mother saw that she could do nothing with him, so she gave him a piece of dry bread and a flask of water, and shoved him out of the house.

The fool went on and on. At last he met an old man, and they stopped to greet each other.

The old man asked the fool, "Where are you going?"

"Well now," said the fool, all excited, "the Tsar

has promised to give his daughter to anyone who can make a ship that can fly."

"And can you make such a ship?"

"No, I cannot, but somewhere I will get it made."

"And where is that somewhere?"

"Heaven only knows."

"Well, now, sit down. Rest and eat a bit. Take out what you have in your knapsack."

"Oh, but it is such poor food that I am ashamed to show it."

"Nonsense! Take it out! What God has given is quite good enough."

The fool undid his knapsack. He could not believe his eyes! There, instead of the dry crust of bread, lay soft white rolls and savory meats. Gladly he shared them with the old man.

So they ate together, and the old man said to the fool, "Go into the wood, right up to the first tree, and cross yourself three times. Next you must strike the tree with your ax, fall with your face to the ground, and wait until someone wakes you. Then you will see before you a ship. You may sit in it and fly wherever you like. But be sure to take on board anyone you meet on your way!"

The fool blessed the old man and said farewell. Going into the wood, he went right up to the first tree and did exactly as he had been told. He crossed himself three times before he struck the tree with his ax. Then he lay down with his face to the ground, and went to sleep.

In a little while someone woke him, and he sat up. There before him was a ship! Without thinking long about it, the fool climbed in. Up into air the ship rose, and it flew on and on.

When the fool looked down, he saw on the road below a man lying with his ear to the damp earth.

"Good day, Uncle!"

"Good day."

"What are you doing?"

"I am listening to what is going on in the world."

"Do come and fly in the ship with me."

The Listener did not want to refuse, so he climbed aboard. On and on the two flew together.

Soon they looked down to the ground. There they saw a man hopping along on one leg, with the other tied tightly to his ear.

"Good day, Uncle, why are you hopping on one leg?"

"Why, if I were to untie the other I could be halfway around the world in a single stride."

"Do come and fly with us."

Swift-of-Foot climbed aboard, and they flew on and on.

Again they looked below. There they saw a man standing with a gun and taking aim.

"Good day, Uncle. At what are you aiming? There is not a bird in sight."

"What! I could hit a bird or beast a hundred leagues away. That's what I call shooting!"

"Please come and fly with us."

The Marksman joined them, and they flew on and on.

Once more they looked down. Now they saw a man carrying on his back a whole sackload of bread.

"Good day, Uncle. Where are you going?"

"I am going to get some bread for dinner."

"But you've got a whole sackload on your back."

"That! Why, I could eat all that in a single mouthful."

"Do come and fly with us."

The Gobbler climbed aboard, and they went flying on and on.

When they looked down now they saw a man walking around a lake.

"Good day, Uncle, what are you looking for?"

"I want to drink, but I can find no water."

"But there's a whole lake before you. Why don't you have a drink of it?"

"That! Why, that water would not be more than a mouthful to me."

"Then do come and fly with us."

The Drinker climbed aboard, and they flew on and on.

Again they looked down. There was a man walking into the forest, and on his shoulders he carried a bundle of wood.

"Good day, Uncle, why are you taking wood to the forest?"

"This is not common wood."

"What sort of wood is it, then?"

"It is so remarkable that if you scatter pieces of this wood, a whole army will spring up."

"Do fly with us then."

The Wood-gatherer joined them, and they flew on and on.

They looked down once more, and this time they saw a man carrying a sack of straw.

"Good day, Uncle. Where are you carrying that straw?"

"To the village."

"Is there no straw in the village, then?"

"Yes, but this is rare and wonderful straw. If you scatter it on the hottest summer day, the day will become cold at once with snow and frost."

"Won't you fly with us, then?"

"Thank you, I will," said the Straw-carrier.

Soon they flew into the courtyard of the Tsar's palace. The Tsar was dining just then, but he heard the flying ship. He was much surprised! He sent his servant out to ask who was flying that ship. The servant brought back word that it was only a poor peasant.

The Tsar fell to thinking. He did not like the idea of giving his lovely daughter to a simple peasant, and so he began to consider how he could settle with him. He decided, "I will give him many impossible tasks to do."

Immediately the Tsar had a servant order the fool to bring him, as soon as the imperial meal was over, some singing water from the end of the world.

Now the first man whom the fool had met (the one who had been listening to what was going on in the world) heard what the Tsar was saying to the servant, and told it to the fool.

"What shall I do now?" asked the fool. "Why, if I should search for a year, and even for my whole life, I would never find such water."

"Don't be afraid," said Swift-of-Foot, his second friend. "I'll manage it for you."

The servant came and made known the Tsar's command.

"Tell the Tsar I shall fetch the water," replied the fool.

Swift-of-Foot untied his other leg from his ear and ran off. In a twinkling he came to the end of the world, where he found the singing water.

"I must make haste to return," said he. But, instead, he sat down under a water mill and went to sleep.

The Tsar's dinner was drawing to a close. Still Swift-of-Foot did not return, and those on board the ship grew uneasy.

The Listener lay down, ear to the ground. "Oh, ho! So you are asleep beneath the mill, are you?"

The Marksman took up his gun. He aimed at the mill and awoke Swift-of-Foot with his shooting.

Swift-of-Foot ran, and in a moment brought the water, just before the Tsar rose from his table.

But the singing water was not enough to satisfy the Tsar. He bade his servant say to the fool, "Come. Since you are so clever, show me that you and your comrades can eat at one meal twenty roasted oxen and twenty loaves of bread."

Listener heard this and told it to the fool.

The fool was terrified. "Why, I can't eat even one loaf at a meal!"

"Don't be afraid," said Gobbler. "That will be very little for me."

The servant came and gave the Tsar's command.

"Good!" said the fool. "Let us have the food and we'll eat it."

The Tsar's men then brought twenty roasted oxen, and twenty loaves of bread.

Gobbler alone ate it all!

"Ugh!" he said. "Precious little. They might have given us a *little* more!"

Now the Tsar ordered the fool to drink forty barrels of wine. Each barrel was to hold forty buckets.

The Listener heard these words and told them to the fool.

The fool was horrified. "Why, I could not drink even one bucketful!"

"Don't be frightened," said the Drinker. "I'll drink for all. It will be little enough for me."

The Tsar's men poured out forty barrels of wine. The Drinker came and swallowed it all at one gulp. "Ugh! Little enough, too," he said. "I should have liked as much more again."

After that the Tsar commanded the fool to go to the bathhouse to make himself ready for his wedding.

Now this bathhouse was made of cast iron, and the Tsar commanded that it should be heated scalding hot. He intended that the fool should be boiled in a single instant.

The fool was frightened. But as he went into the bathhouse, the Straw-carrier followed him. They were both locked in.

Now the fool's friend scattered his straw, and at once the water in the bath froze so hard that the fool was scarcely able to wash himself. He crept up onto the stove and spent the night there. In the morning when the servants unlocked the bathhouse, they found the fool alive and well, lying on the stove and singing happily.

★ ★ ★

The Tsar was puzzled. He did not know how

to rid himself of this fool. He thought and thought. At last he commanded the fool to collect a whole army of his own soldiers—for, thought he, how will a simple peasant be able to form an army? Certainly he will not be able to do *that*.

The fool heard this new command with alarm. "Now I am lost," said he. "You have saved me more than once, my friends, but it is plain that you can do nothing now."

"You're a fine fellow," said the man with the bundle of wood. "Why, you've forgotten all about me, haven't you?"

The servant came and gave the fool the Tsar's command. "If you will have his daughter, you must have a whole army on foot by morning."

"I agree," said the fool. "But if the Tsar, even after this, should refuse, I will conquer his whole kingdom and take his daughter by force."

At night the Wood-gatherer went out into the fields. He began scattering his sticks in all directions. Immediately a great army sprang up, with some soldiers on horse and some on foot.

In the morning the Tsar saw the army standing on all sides. Now it was the Tsar's turn to be terrified. Without wasting a minute, he had his men carry gifts of rare gems and fine clothing to the fool. And he ordered his men to bring the fool to court. The fool would be married to the Tsarevna.

The fool attired himself in the costly garments, which made him more handsome than words can describe. Then he came before the Tsar.

He married the beautiful Tsarevna, who came to love him as he loved her, and they lived together happily for many long years.

About This Series

I N RECENT DECADES, folk tales and fairy tales from all corners of the earth have been made available in a variety of handsome collections and in lavishly illustrated picture books. But in the 1950s, such a rich selection was not yet available. The classic fairy and folk tales were most often found in cumbersome books with small print and few illustrations. Helen Jones, then children's book editor at Little, Brown and Company, accepted a proposal from a Boston librarian for an ambitious series with a simple goal — to put an international selection of stories into the hands of children. The tales would be published in slim volumes, with wide margins and ample leading, and illustrated by a cast of contemporary artists. The result was a unique series of books intended for children to read by themselves — the Favorite Fairy Tales series. Available only in hardcover for many years, the books have now been reissued in paperbacks that feature new illustrations and covers.

The series embraces the stories of sixteen different

countries: France, England, Germany, India, Ireland, Sweden, Poland, Russia, Spain, Czechoslovakia, Scotland, Greece, Japan, Denmark, Italy, and Norway. Some of these stories may seem violent or fantastical to our modern sensibilities, yet they often reflect the deepest yearnings and imaginings of the human mind and heart.

Virginia Haviland traveled abroad frequently and was able to draw upon librarians, storytellers, and writers in countries as far away as Japan to help make her selections. But she was also an avid researcher with a keen interest in rare books, and most of the stories she included in the series were found through a diligent search of old collections. Ms. Haviland was associated with the Boston Public Library for nearly thirty years—as a children's and branch librarian, and eventually as Readers Advisor to Children. She reviewed for *The Horn Book Magazine* for almost thirty years and in 1963 was named Head of the Children's Book Section of the Library of Congress. Ms. Haviland remained with the Library of Congress for nearly twenty years and wrote and lectured about children's literature throughout her career. She died in 1988.